Other Tippy Bear books by Coby Hol

Tippy Bear Goes to a Party
Tippy Bear Hunts for Honey
Tippy Bear and Little Sam

First published in the United States, Great Britain, Canada,
Australia and New Zealand in 1992 by North-South Books,
an imprint of Nord-Süd Verlag AG, Gossau Zürich, Switzerland.

Distributed in the United States by North-South Books Inc., New York.

Library of Congress Cataloging-in-Publication Data
Hol, Coby
Tippy Bear's Christmas / written and illustrated by Coby Hol.
Summary: Tippy Bear makes two new animal friends,
who help him celebrate Christmas.
ISBN 1-55858-156-1 (trade binding)
ISBN 1-55858-157-X (library binding)
[1. Christmas—Fiction.   2. Bears—Fiction.
3. Animals—Fiction.]   I. Title
PZ7.H688Tp   1992
[E]—dc20   91-45679

British Library Cataloguing in Publication Data
Hol, Coby
Tippy Bear's Christmas
I. Title
823   [J]
ISBN 1-55858-156-1

1 3 5 7 9 10 8 6 4 2
Printed in Belgium

Tippy Bear's Christmas

Written and Illustrated by Coby Hol

North-South Books
New York

"Good morning," said Tippy Bear to the bird in the window. "I'm glad you woke me up. I have a lot to do today. Tomorrow is Christmas! My parents are shopping in the village. I'm going to get everything ready by myself."

Tippy made honey cakes using his mother's recipe. When he had baked a whole mountain of honey cakes, he said to himself: "So many cakes! Mama will be very happy, but we can't eat them all!"

Tippy looked for some gold paper, scissors and paste. Then he made a Christmas star. When the star was finished, he hung it in the window.

From the attic Tippy fetched a big box full of Christmas ornaments. He was very careful not to drop the box. Most of the ornaments were made of glass.

"Oh, how beautiful!" said Tippy, as he unpacked the glass balls.

Tippy went out to the garden with a big saw
to look for a Christmas tree. He looked
carefully until he found the perfect tree.

"Why have you sawed down that tree?"
asked the hedgehog.
"Tomorrow is Christmas, and I'm going to
decorate this tree with ornaments," said Tippy.

"Christmas? What's that?" asked the hedgehog.

"It's the most beautiful holiday in the whole year!" said Tippy. "Come with me, and we'll celebrate it together."

"That sounds like fun," said the hedgehog. "I don't feel like hibernating yet."

"I've baked a great big pile of honey cakes," said Tippy, as they carried the tree back to the house.

Tippy and the hedgehog took great care with the decorations.

"These ornaments make the tree look so lovely," said the hedgehog.

"Just wait until my parents get home and put candles on the tree," said Tippy.

Tippy looked up and saw that the little bird
was once again perched in the window.

"How wonderful that you're visiting us,"
said Tippy, letting it in. "Come and have some
milk and honey cakes."

"Do you celebrate Christmas every year?" asked the hedgehog.

"Of course," said Tippy. "I hope you can come back next year."

"I'd love to," said the hedgehog with a smile.

At last, Tippy's parents came home. His mother had presents under her arm.

"Look what I found in the garden," said Tippy's father with a laugh, holding up the saw.

"The tree looks beautiful," said Tippy's mother, "and I see you've made some new friends."

Tippy's father put candles on the tree and carefully lit them one by one.

"What a beautiful sight," said the hedgehog.

"Thank you for inviting us," chirped the bird.

"My pleasure," said Tippy. "You've made this the best Christmas ever!"